THE SNOW GIANT

by Peyo

Ready-to-Read

Simon Spotlight/Nickelodeon

New York   London   Toronto   Sydney

SIMON SPOTLIGHT

An imprint of Simon & Schuster Children's Publishing Division
1230 Avenue of the Americas, New York, New York 10020
© Peyo - 2011 - Licensed through Lafig Belgium - www.smurf.com
All rights reserved, including the right of
reproduction in whole or in part in any form.
SIMON SPOTLIGHT, READY-TO-READ,
and colophon are registered
trademarks of Simon & Schuster, Inc.
For information about special discounts for bulk purchases,
please contact Simon & Schuster Special Sales at
1-866-506-1949 or business@simonandschuster.com.
Manufactured in the United States of America 1111 LAK.
4 5 6 7 8 9 10
ISBN 978-1-4424-2892-8 (pbk)
ISBN 978-1-4424-3610-7 (hc)
based on the book *L'Abominable créature des neiges*

The Smurfs were working
on the Smurf River dam when
an accident happened. A log
fell on Papa Smurf's foot!

"Oh, it hurts!" cried Papa Smurf.
"My foot is starting to swell.
I need some pollen from the
snow flower to make it better."

"We'll get it!" said Brainy and
Clumsy. They ran to Papa's house
to get the jar of pollen.
On the way back, Clumsy tripped.
The jar fell into the river!

"Sorry, Papa," said Clumsy.
"We will get more pollen!" said Brainy.
"It will not be easy," Papa said.
"There is only one snow flower,
and it grows on Ice Mountain."

Brainy wanted to help,
even though he was scared.
"We can do it!" he said.
Soon, Brainy and a team of Smurfs
left to find the snow flower.

The brave little Smurfs began
to climb up the steep mountain,
but a cold, gusty wind
made it very hard!

Smurfette slid further down
the mountain than the other Smurfs.
She slid all the way to the edge
and flew into the air!

Smurfette felt like she was
falling for a very long time.
She closed her eyes and tried
not to think about landing!

The Smurfs were too busy climbing to notice a strange, white creature watching them from above.

Suddenly, Brainy fell down!
"I am fine," he said. "But why
are there so many holes in the
ground?"

What the Smurfs did not know
was that the holes in the ground
were actually footprints!
Someone with very big feet
had walked in the snow!

The Smurfs almost made it to
the top of the mountain and saw
the scarlet snow flower growing
on the peak. It was very high up.
How would they reach it?

The Smurfs worked together to help Smurfette climb to the top. Smurfette had the snow flower in her hand!

Then one Smurf slipped
and they all fell down.

But instead of hard,
snowy ground,
she landed on a
large, soft hand.

It was the Snow Giant! He caught
Smurfette and saved her! Then he
brought her back to his cave,
and even made a little fur coat
to keep her warm.

The Snow Giant really wanted her to stay, but Smurfette said no. "Thank you for saving me," said Smurfette. "But I cannot stay here. I miss Smurf Village and want to go home."

The Smurfs were worried about
Smurfette. Where could she be?

"We have to go smurf some help!"
said Brainy. "But how?"
Then he had an idea....

The Smurfs made a fire
at their campsite. Maybe Papa Smurf
would see the smoke and help them!
The Snow Giant saw the fire and
ran over to stomp it out.
He did not like fire!
He liked ice and snow.

When the Snow Giant ran back
to his cave, the Smurfs heard
Smurfette calling for help.
"She is in there!" they cheered.
But the Snow Giant would
not let her leave.

When Papa Smurf saw the smoke,
he knew there must be trouble
on the mountain.
Papa Smurf and a troop of Smurfs
came right away to help.

First Papa healed his foot with
the pollen, and then he came up
with a plan.
"The Snow Giant is scared of fire,"
he said. "Let's each smurf a torch
and save Smurfette!"

It worked! When the Snow Giant saw the torches he was scared and ran farther into his cave, taking Smurfette with him.

"Don't smurf him!" pleaded
Smurfette. "He is just lonely."
"If Smurfette stays, she will die,"
said Papa to the Snow
Giant, "just like the
last snow flower."

Hearing this, the Snow Giant led the
Smurfs to a cave full of snow flowers!
"It's smurftastic!" cheered the Smurfs.

"We are going to have a great harvest of pollen this year," said Papa Smurf. "Thanks to our new friend!"

"Do not worry," said Smurfette to
the kind Snow Giant. "We will see
each other every year when
we come here for more pollen.
We will not forget you!"

The Snow Giant had tears in his eyes.
He finally had friends!

"See you next year!" the Smurfs cried
as they headed home.
"That gives me enough time to knit
him a pretty scarf," said Smurfette.